Clifford

Goes to Kindergarten

Norman Bridwell

SCHOLASTIC INC.

ISBN 978-0-545-82335-7

10 9 8   20 21 22 23/0

Printed in the U.S.A.   40
This edition first printing, April 2019

Hello! My name is Emily Elizabeth, and this is my dog, Clifford.
I started kindergarten yesterday.
At first I was scared, but now I love school.

Before school started, my mom read me a book about what my first day of kindergarten would be like. She said I would make lots of new friends and learn all about writing, counting, animals, and my neighborhood.

We went to see my new school. Clifford stayed outside, but just knowing he was close by made me feel better.

We met my teacher, Ms. Tate, and she showed
us around the classroom. She was very nice.

We visited the nurse's office. If I ever
feel sick, the nurse will take care of me.

Later, we played school in my backyard. I was the teacher, and my mom and Clifford were my students. I tried to be just like Ms. Tate.

I still had a few questions for my mom. I asked her what would happen
if I missed home, or if I didn't make any friends.
She said that Ms. Tate would help me feel better if I was sad. She would
also make sure I didn't have to play by myself.

The next day, Clifford and I were playing hide-and-seek when a letter came in the mail. It was from my teacher.

The letter said that each kindergartner could bring something from home to school on the first day to help make them feel comfortable. I knew exactly what to bring!

On the first day of kindergarten, Ms. Tate greeted us at the classroom door. She was very surprised to see Clifford. All the other kids brought stuffed animals, toys, or blankets. They all smiled when they saw Clifford.

It was time for school to start. I said good-bye to my mom.

We all sat in a circle, and Ms. Tate taught us a welcome song.

Clifford tried to sing along, too, but all he could do was howl.

Then we all took turns going to the front of the class to answer a question on the board. Ms. Tate asked the question, and we wrote yes or no.

Even Clifford had a turn!

We practiced writing letters and words. Some kids were nervous about writing. Clifford gave them kisses to help them feel better.

Unfortunately, his kisses were very slobbery!

Next, Ms. Tate asked us to paint a picture of home.

Clifford missed home as much as I did. When he saw my painting he started wagging his tail really fast. OOPS! He knocked over some of the water and paint with his tail.

Clifford rolled around on the floor to try and clean it up.

Finally, it was time for lunch. I was so hungry!
So was Clifford.

Everyone loved Clifford so much they wanted to give him treats. But Ms. Tate said we needed to eat our own food so we could have energy for the rest of the school day.

At recess everyone wanted to play with Clifford.
We made a lot of friends on the playground.

Clifford's tail is a great jump rope.
And his nose is the best slide!

At naptime, we were all tired from playing outside.
But we weren't used to sleeping on the rug.
It was hard to get comfortable.

That's when Clifford had an idea!

Clifford let everyone snuggle up with him. Soon we all fell fast asleep. Ms. Tate was happy we were able to nap. We still had a long school day ahead of us.

Clifford saved naptime! We woke up ready for the rest of the school day.

Bringing Clifford to my first day of kindergarten was a big success!
I can't wait to go back to school tomorrow.